YOU GO FIRST

By MERCER MAYER

"So in everything, do to others what you would have them do to you"
Matthew 7:12

You Go First

© 2013 by Mercer Mayer

Published in Nashville, Tennessee, by Tommy Nelson. Tommy Nelson is a registered trademark of Thomas Nelson, Inc.

Little Critter, Mercer Mayer's Little Critter and Mercer Mayer's Little Critter and Logo are trademarks of Orchard House Licensing Company. All rights reserved.

Tommy Nelson titles may be purchased in bulk for educational, business, fund-raising, or sales promotional use. For information, please e-mail SpecialMarkets@ThomasNelson.com.

Scripture quotations are taken from *The International Children's Bible*®. © 1986, 1988, 1999 by Thomas Nelson, Inc. All rights reserved.

Library of Congress Cataloging-in-Publication Data

Mayer, Mercer, 1943- author, illustrator.

You go first : so in everything, do to others what you would have them do to you, Matthew 7:12 / by Mercer Mayer.

pages cm

Summary: "Litter Critter loves being first--even if it hurts his family and friends. After several missteps, Little Critter learns that the secret to getting along is treating others the way he wants to be treated--which, in Little Critter's case, means letting someone else be first"-- Provided by publisher.

ISBN 978-1-4003-2245-9 (softcover : alk. paper) [1. Golden rule--Fiction. 2. Conduct of life--Fiction. 3. Christian life--Fiction.] I. Title.

PZ7.M462Yl 2013

[E]--dc23

2013008972

Printed in China

13 14 15 16 17 LEO 6 5 4 3 2 1

www.littlecritter.com

Today I helped Dad put up a new swing in our backyard.
I really wanted to be the first to try it, but Little Sister
got to go first instead. It's not fair!

Mom made smiley face pancakes for breakfast and I helped. I wanted to have the first pancake, but Mom told me to give it to my baby brother because he's the littlest.

I never get to be first.

I wanted to be first on the school bus. I didn't mean to bump into Gabby. It was just an accident. But I did get to go first!

At snack, I thought Tiger might beat me to it, but I got the first milk. Hooray!

And at recess, I was first on the trampoline even though Gator might have been there one teensy second before me.

When it was time for Show and Tell, I jumped up instead of raising my hand. "Me first please, Miss Kitty!" I said.

I was so excited I kind of dropped my Show and Tell. It took a while to get the ants to go back to their farm. There was no more time for anyone else to do their Show and Tells. Oops!

Miss Kitty made a special announcement when school was over. She said there was going to be a class picnic with games and races and everything. "I hope I come in first and win a prize," I said.

"Little Critter, having fun isn't about being first," said Miss Kitty. "It's about enjoying time with your friends and family and appreciating them just as you like them to appreciate you.

God tells us in the Bible that we should treat others the way we want to be treated. Sometimes that means letting them go first. That shows you care, and caring is the secret to getting along."

After school we went to Tiger's house to scooter up these new ramps his dad built. "I call first!" I said. But Gator said Tiger should go first, because it was his house.

"You know what, Little Critter?" said Gabby. "You were more fun when you didn't always have to be first."

When it was my turn, you know what happened? I wiped out. I bet I wouldn't have wiped out if I went first.

At the picnic Gator was my partner in the three-legged race. "We have to come in first," I said.

"Remember, this race is about working together," said Miss Kitty. "On your marks, get set, go!"

I hopped way faster than Gator and before I knew it, we both fell down. Gator said it was because we weren't working together. I said it was because he wasn't hopping fast enough.

Next was the egg and spoon relay. I got to go first.
Hooray! But I ran so fast, the egg kind of fell off the spoon,
so the other team won.

Then it was time to eat. "Who wants the first hot dog?" asked Miss Kitty.

"Me, me, me!" I said.

"All you care about is being first," said Gator. "You're not being a good friend."

Gator was wrong. I was so a good friend. I just liked to go first.

For the scavenger hunt, we had to find a stick, a rock, and an acorn. Sticks and rocks were easy to find, but nobody could find an acorn. While everyone else talked with their teams, I spotted a bunch of trees that I bet had acorns. I ran fast so I could get there first.

It was dark in the woods and very quiet. Suddenly, I heard something. It was a snake! I was so scared, I couldn't move. I really, really wished someone else could go first.

But I was all by myself, because I'd run away from everyone just so I could be first. Gator was right. I wasn't a good friend at all.

The snake hissed. Aaahh!!! I ran as fast as I could go!

When I got back to the picnic, I was so happy to see my friends I didn't care if I ever went first again! I thought about what Mrs. Kitty said about how we should treat others. I wanted to show my friends I cared by treating them the way I would want to be treated. Gator won the scavenger hunt and I cheered really loud.

When it was time to get on the bus, I said, "You go first."
So Gabby went first.

At school even though I was first at the slide, I said to
Timothy, "You go first!" He gave me a big smile.

And when we lined up to go in from recess, I said
to Gator, "You go first!" even though I was line leader.
Gator smiled.

"You go first," I said to Henrietta at the water fountain.

At home, Little Sister and I both wanted to go on the swing. I said, "You go first." And I even pushed her.

Every time I say to someone, "You go first," you know what happens? They smile. And that makes me feel really good! It's the way I show my friends and family I care about them, just like the Bible says, and that truly is the secret to getting along!